P9-DCO-850

No Ordinary Olive

by ROBERTA BAKER

Illustrated by DEBBIE TILLEY

Little, Brown and Company
Boston New York London

For Isabel
I still love you bigger than space.
PGFWABF

And for my father, Edward A. Baker
Thank you for all your gifts.
— R. B.

For Gillian
— D. T.

Text copyright © 2002 by Roberta Baker
Illustrations copyright © 2002 by Debbie Tilley

First Edition

Library of Congress Cataloging-in-Publication Data
Baker, Roberta.
   No ordinary Olive / by Roberta Baker ; illustrated by Debbie Tilley. — 1st ed.
   p. cm.
   Summary: From the day she is born, Olive, an exuberant young girl, enjoys life in her
own way and even though she is occasionally misunderstood, her parents support her.
   ISBN 0-316-07336-9
   [1. Individuality — Fiction. 2. Parent and child — Fiction.] I. Tilley, Debbie, ill. II. Title.
   PZ7.B17485 No 2001
   [E] — dc21   00-044391

10 9 8 7 6 5 4 3 2 1

TWP

Printed in Singapore

The illustrations for this book were done in watercolor and ink.
The text was set in Fairfield and Providence, and the title was handlettered by Holly Dickens.

When Olive Elizabeth Julia Jerome was born, she cried louder than any other baby.

"What pitch!" raved her mother.

Olive wailed at the top of her lungs in a language no one could understand:

Hello, great big world! It's me, Olive. Hey, where does a baby get

One morning, after pouring out cereal, she surprised her parents with breakfast in bed.

Cock-a-doodle-doo! Rise and shine, Mom and Dad!
Last one to eat is a hard-boiled egg!

Olive's mother rubbed her eyes and gasped. "Oatmeal — with pickles!"
Olive's father gulped. "With bubble gum–raisin pancakes on the side."

On sunny days, Olive played outdoors. She slid as fast as she could down the highest slide. She hurled Gumbo, her stuffed bear, into the sky with such force that he almost went into orbit.

Here you go, Gumbo! Hitch a ride on a rocket! Be the first polar bear to prowl in space, and bring back some moon rocks for Mom!

"Oh, my, my, my," said Olive's Aunt Tiffany. She liked to sew lacy dresses for Olive's dolls and was shocked to see them on Gumbo.

"How revolutionary!" piped Olive's mother. "A party dress that converts to a parachute!"

"She's no ordinary Olive." Olive's father beamed. "Maybe she'll be an astronaut, a test pilot, a stunt driver . . ."

When Olive went swimming at the pond in summer, she did not float and flutter her feet. She flapped like a seal, barked like a walrus, and dove like an otter to the mud bottom, where she searched for pirate treasure, sunken toy ships, and pearls in the mouths of make-believe oysters.

Ahoy, matey! Make way, landlubber! Pirate Olive coming aboard.
Hoist this treasure, Blackbeard — or you'll swab the deck and eat liver!

School was a chance to try something different.

"Sweetheart, remember: Pay attention," her parents reminded her. "And do

Olive tried to be good—very good. In fact, most of the time she was

But when Ms. Fishbone's class practiced the alphabet on dotted lines, Olive thought it would be more fun to pretend the lines were railroad tracks. She imagined her letters were cars on a train. She raced her W's, X's, Y's, and Z's until they crashed, piled up, grew taller and wider, and spread to workbooks all over the room.

Olive looked around. "Uh-oh . . ."

Ms. Fishbone made Olive write her name forty-seven times on the blackboard.

The class giggled.

"That will do," Ms. Fishbone said.

She took Olive to visit the school principal.

"Olive, why can't you behave like everyone else?" Mr. Weepole asked. "Why do you have to be different?"

Olive thought about it and answered, "But Mr. Weepole, I like being different. It's the way I am."

Olive sat alone in the principal's office, practicing letters in her workbook. She stared at the gray file cabinets, the padlocked supply closets, and Mr. Weepole's empty desk.

"No wonder Mr. Weepole isn't happy. I know how to cheer him up. I'll redecorate!"

Olive took out her crayons, markers, and paints. She drew boa constrictors and Bengal tigers and hairy-chested gorillas and spider monkeys and howler monkeys swinging on vines between trees. . . .

"*My desk!*" bellowed Mr. Weepole when he walked into his office. "You've turned my desk into a jungle, Miss Jerome!"

"How expressive!" gushed the art teacher.

"What a bold statement!" gabbed the drama teacher.

"What a unique science project," trumpeted the science teacher. "May I borrow this desk for my 'Life in a Rain Forest' lesson?"

"Mr. Weepole," tooted the music teacher, "I think this desk might win the school decorating contest!"

Mr. Weepole turned salmon pink, then maroon. Olive thought smoke would pour from his nostrils.

"Miss Jerome . . . don't you know that you shouldn't . . . *decorate* . . . things that belong to other people?!"

The teachers stared at Olive.

Olive sputtered, "I-I know, Mr. Weepole. But I wanted to surprise you. I wanted to show you that if you paint something a brighter color, you'll see the world a new way."

"She's right, Mr. Weepole," chimed the school nurse. "Take two aspirin and stare at that desk. It will help you relax. It might even make you smile."

"Smile? *Smile?* Who says I don't *smile?*"

The nurse and teachers and Olive stared at Mr. Weepole.

Mr. Weepole paced the room, digging his fists into his pockets. "All right," he muttered. "I'll keep the desk. On one condition . . ." He took a deep breath and adjusted his tie. "That Olive Elizabeth Julia Jerome obeys Ms. Fishbone and follows the rules here at Stickler Street School. And if she wants to do something *really* different, *she asks for permission first!*"

Olive jumped up and down, shouting, "Yippee!" She sang:

Wake up, world! Paint everything a brighter color! Then turn your paint box into a ship. Chart a course for someplace you've never been. Who knows what you'll discover?!

Today, when Olive goes to school or out to play, she tries to be patient, gentle, and calm — everything that grown-ups tell her to be.

Most of the time, she is gentle and calm. But it's hard to be patient with the world racing by.

Each night, when it's time to sleep, Olive snuggles under the covers just like other kids. She hugs her polar bear, kisses her mom and dad. Then she whispers after they turn out the light:

Hello, stars! It's me, remember? Olive Elizabeth Julia Jerome! I'm building a spaceship now. It won't be long before . . .

"Good night, dear Olive," says her mother, opening the door and blowing a kiss.

"Good night, No Ordinary Olive," says her father. "We love you with all our heart."